FIGHTING FORCES ON THE SEA

FRIGATES

LYNN M. STONE

Rourke
Publishing LLC
Vero Beach, Florida 32964

www.rourkepublishing.com

PHOTO CREDITS: All photos courtesy of the U.S. Navy except p. 22, 23, 24, 25 courtesy of the Naval Institute

Title page: *In the control center, crewmen guide the guided missile frigate* Vandergrift *safely through the ocean.*

Editor: Frank Sloan

Library of Congress Cataloging-in-Publication Data

Stone, Lynn M.
Frigates / Lynn M. Stone.
p. cm. -- (Fighting forces on the sea)
Includes bibliographical references and index.
ISBN 1-59515-465-5 (hardcover)

Printed in the USA

CG/CG

Rourke Publishing

www.rourkepublishing.com – sales@rourkepublishing.com
Post Office Box 3328, Vero Beach, FL 32964
1-800-394-7055

Table of Contents

★ Frigates

The U.S. Navy's guided missile frigates are the smallest of its "surface **combatants**." Surface combatants are warships that operate on the ocean surface and have the capability to defend themselves as well as to attack. Aircraft carriers, for instance, technically are not surface combatants because they depend largely on other ships—like guided missile frigates—for their protection.

Active guided missile frigates, all of which belong to the *Oliver Hazard Perry* **class**, are the smallest of U.S. surface combatants. The largest surface combatants in the U.S. Navy are *Ticonderoga*-class guided missile **cruisers**, followed by *Arleigh Burke*-class guided missile **destroyers**, and *Spruance*-class destroyers.

▲
Guided missile frigates, like the USS Doyle, *shown here in the Caribbean Sea, are the smallest of the Navy's major surface warships.*

▲
Part of the carrier Carl Vinson *Battle Group, the guided missile frigate* Ingraham *(far left) undergoes at-sea refueling from the fast combat support ship USS* Sacramento.

Of course, being "small" among surface warships is a little like being "only" 6 feet 2 inches (1.9 meters) on an NBA court. The frigates are 453 feet (138 meters) in length, which makes them longer than a football field (360 feet, or 110 meters).

American guided missile frigates, designated FFG, have been part of the Navy since 1977. They were designed during the Cold War (1945-1991) with the former Soviet Union. Their jobs were to serve as escort vessels for groups of naval ships, such as amphibious expeditionary forces, convoys, and battle forces. The guided missile frigates were built chiefly to combat enemy submarines. But they were also designed to have at least a secondary role as antiaircraft ships. In recent years frigates have sometimes been used to counter drug smuggling and intercept vessels for search.

FACT FILE ★

From the U.S. Navy: "It is important to note that hull number letter prefixes are not acronyms and should not be treated as abbreviations of ship type classifications. Thus DD does not stand for anything more than Destroyer. SS simply means Submarine. And FF, the post-1975 type code for Frigate most emphatically, is not translated as 'Fast Frigate.' "

▲

The Thach, *like other guided missile frigates, was built chiefly as an escort vessel and to combat enemy submarines.*

The end of the Cold War allowed the United States to streamline and downsize the Navy. But the U.S. Navy has remained the world's most powerful navy by upgrading its Cold War-era ships and **commissioning** newer, better ships.

Perry-class frigates have been modernized several times with better weapons and weapons systems. The addition, for instance, of features such as LAMPS III-equipped SH-60B Seahawk helicopters have given the ships far more combat strength than anyone could have imagined in 1977.

FACT FILE 

THE LATEST SHIPS OF THE *PERRY* CLASS HAVE FULLY LOADED **DISPLACEMENTS** OF 4,100 TONS (3,737 METRIC TONS). THEY WERE DESIGNED FOR 3,600 TONS (3,276 METRIC TONS), OR CLOSE TO IT. THE ADDED WEIGHT HAS NOT HELPED THE SHIPS' STABILITY.

▲

The addition of LAMPS III-equipped helicopters to guided missile frigates have helped keep them useful long after their introduction in 1977.

But like all types of military hardware, ships eventually become **obsolete**. Their **hulls** and **superstructures** age, and their design may not be compatible with the most advanced weapons and electronics. They simply cannot "grow" any more. In the case of guided missile frigates, they lack the capability to perform the several kinds of missions that the Navy requires of its latest cruisers and destroyers.

Despite nearly three decades of upgrades—or because of them to some extent—the *Perry*-class ships will gradually be phased out. The last of the 55 ships in the class, the USS *Ingraham*, was commissioned in 1989.

FACT FILE ★

By 2005, the Navy had reduced the number of active *Perrys* to 22, and some of those were in the U.S. Naval Reserve.

▲
The USS Rueben James, *one of the 30 operational guided missile frigates of the U.S. Navy, leads two Pakistan Navy ships on a joint naval exercise.*

New systems added to older ship designs can create unforeseen problems. As new systems have been added to *Perry*-class ships, their displacements have grown, so the ships carry more weight than was intended.

In 2003 the Navy began removing the MK-13 guided missile launchers from the remaining *Perry*-class ships. The Navy explained the decision by noting the advanced age of the launcher. The MK-13 system is not effective against the latest high-speed cruise missiles. Ironically, it left FFG ships without the G—as in guided missile!

But the *Perrys* weren't left toothless. They have other weapons, and upgrades to the remaining *Perrys* continue. The ships will replace their Phalanx Close-In Weapons Systems, for example, with a more advanced version. They will also receive a new missile decoy system that will counter the loss of their guided missiles.

Frigate Specifications

Guided Missile Frigate

Powerplant:
2 gas turbine engines, 1 shaft; 41,000 shaft horsepower

Length:
445 feet (133.5 meters) with LAMPS III modifications

Beam:
45 feet (13.5 meters)

Displacement:
4,100 tons (3,791 metric tons) fully loaded

Speed:
29+ knots (33.4 miles, 53 kilometers per hour)

Aircraft:
2 SH-60 LAMPS III helicopters

Ship's company:
17 officers, 198 enlisted

Armament:
6 MK-46 torpedoes; 1 76mm, 62-caliber MK-75 rapid fire gun; 1 Phalanx Close-In Weapons System

Commissioning date, first ship:
1977

▲
Heavy with the latest technology and weapons systems, guided missile frigates like the USS Elrod *have little room to "grow" with future technology.*

Frigate Characteristics

CHAPTER TWO

An American FFG has a tall, sharp **bow** leading to its long, narrow deck and superstructure. The superstructure houses the ship's company and its command and control functions. It is also a platform for antennas, guns, and electronic surveillance gear.

▲
USS George Philip *is shown firing a surface-to-air missile in 2002.*

The deck **stern** is a port for the ship's two Seahawk helicopters. The two-engine Seahawks are an extension of the ship itself. The twin-engine helicopters extend the ship's ability to detect and combat submarines. Seahawks are also used for search and rescue missions, anti-ship warfare, cargo lift, and special operations.

▲

Guided missile frigates will replace their high-tech Phalanx Close-In Weapons System with an even more advanced version.

Seahawks are equipped with high-tech sound detectors, radar, and torpedoes. The helicopters typically have a crew of three: a pilot, a sensor operator, and an airborne tactical officer. The tactical officer is responsible for "the moment"—deciding which weapons should be used and when. The sensor operator interprets the electronic sensors of the Seahawk, its radar and sound-sensing gear. The sensor operator also coordinates water rescues and therefore must qualify as an exceptional swimmer.

▲
An Aviation warfare systems operator aboard an SH-60B helicopter tracks a surface contact on the Seahawk's radar screen.

Seahawk helicopter crewmen practice cable hoist maneuvers in the western Pacific.

▲
The door gunner aboard an SH-60 Seahawk mans the helicopter's .50-caliber machine gun.

Each Seahawk is equipped with LAMPS III, an **acronym** for Light Airborne Multipurpose System. LAMPS electronics help the Seahawk and the FFG watch, target, and ultimately attack potential enemies, such as other surface ships and submarines.

The FFG's armament includes two triple-mount torpedo launches for MK-46 torpedoes, a 62-caliber MK-75 rapid fire gun, and the Phalanx system, built around highly automated 20-millimeter guns.

FACT FILE ★

THE SEAHAWK CAN BE EQUIPPED WITH PENGUIN MISSILES, THREE MK-46 OR MK-50 TORPEDOES, OR ADDITIONAL 50-CALIBER MACHINE GUNS MOUNTED IN THE CRAFT'S DOORS.

Early History

CHAPTER THREE

The word "frigate" has been in the naval vocabulary since the 17th century. It referred to an unusually fast sailing ship. The most famous American frigate is the well-preserved USS *Constitution*, remembered as "Old Ironsides." *Constitution* was launched in 1797 and fought against the British Royal Navy in the War of 1812.

▲
In a Michel Felice Corne painting from the 19th century, the USS Constitution (right) *is shown approaching the HMS* Guerriere *on August 19, 1812. The American frigate destroyed the British ship.*

Wooden frigates grew larger, faster, and more powerful, although they were never the biggest warships. When steel replaced wood and steam replaced sail in the warships of the late 1800s, "cruiser" replaced "frigate" as a term for large, fast gunships. With the disappearance of the original frigates, the term frigate has been used to describe many different American ships.

FACT FILE ★

THE USS *CONSTITUTION* WAS NICKNAMED "OLD IRONSIDES" REPORTEDLY BECAUSE A SAILOR ABOARD HER NOTICED A BRITISH CANNONBALL BOUNCING OFF HER TOUGH, WOODEN HULL DURING A BATTLE. SHE IS THE OLDEST SHIP STILL IN U.S. NAVY COMMISSION. THE *CONSTITUTION* IS ON PUBLIC DISPLAY IN BOSTON HARBOR.

▲
The USS Pensacola, *photographed in June, 1861, was a Civil War-era frigate.*

CHAPTER FOUR

WORLD WAR II

The term "frigate" resurfaced during World War II in both the U.S. and British Royal navies. America built hundreds of relatively small fighting ships called destroyer escorts (DEs). They were smaller than true destroyers and had only half the power. About 300 feet (91 meters) long and with displacements in the 1,400 to 1,800 ton (1,274 to 1,638 metric ton) range, they were armed with guns and torpedoes. A smaller number of similar ships were built minus the torpedoes. These were called

The destroyer escort England *was a deadly foe of Japanese submarines. It sank 5 in 12 days in 1944 and soon after it helped sink a sixth! On May 9, 1945, a Japanese suicide plane rammed the* England, *killing 37 of her crew, and knocking her out of the war.*

frigates, or patrol frigates, designated PF. Most of them were manned by U.S. Coast Guard crews.

DEs and PFs were used in both the Atlantic and Pacific during World War II. Although they sometimes fired their antiaircraft guns in defense of larger American ships, their primary job was antisubmarine warfare.

▲
World War II destroyer escorts, like the Mason, *were forerunners of more modern frigates. At a time when the U.S. Navy was segregated, the* Mason *was noteworthy: African Americans made up 150 of its 156-man company.*

After World War II

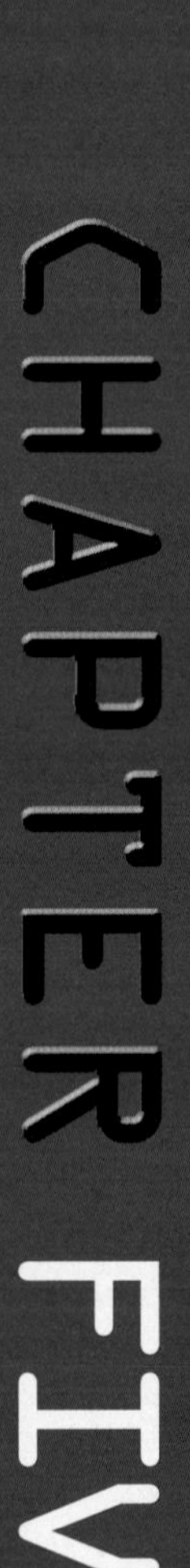

The so-called destroyer escort was the forerunner of the modern frigate. In fact, the Navy renamed some of the destroyer escorts as frigates (FF) in the years after the war. By the mid 1970s all the old DEs and PF ships had been scrapped, sold, or retired.

In 1975 the Navy decided to rename its new antisubmarine escort vessels frigates (FF) and guided missile frigates (FFG). The first post-World War II frigates (FF) were designed in the 1960s and delivered in the 1970s, during the height of the Cold War. These ships were about the same size as the present guided missile frigates. As the new FFG ships came forth, the Navy retired the FF frigates. They were **decommissioned** by the early 1990s.

The destroyer leader frigates (DL) of the late 1950s and early 1960s were yet another class. Because they were larger even than previous destroyers, they were eventually reclassified as destroyers (DDG).

The Navy's bigger-yet, **nuclear**-powered (DLGN) frigates also entered service in the 1960s. They were reclassified, too, as cruisers. They all had been decommissioned by the 1990s.

▲
The present-day guided missile frigates (the USS McClusky *is shown here) replaced the frigates introduced by the U.S. Navy in the 1960s.*

The Future of Frigates

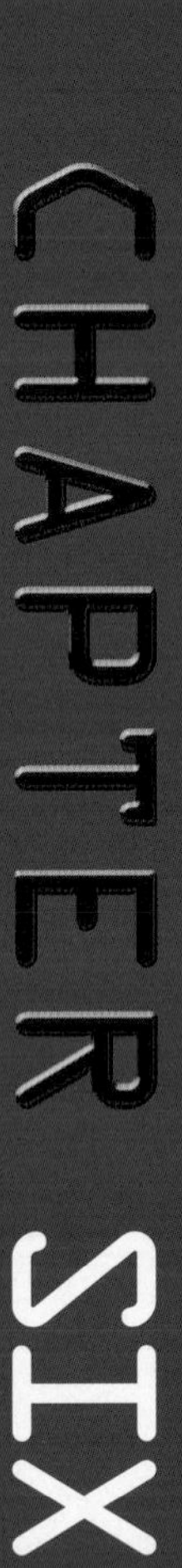

The Navy's escort ships, by every name, have had a long, useful service. Some of the *Perry*-class frigates will remain in commission well beyond 2010. But the Navy has no plans to build any more ships of the frigate type, which are considered "single mission" ships.

▲
Perry-*class frigates will remain in service for several more years.*

American frigates will be replaced by the DD(X) destroyer, which will also replace *Spruance*-class destroyers. The DD(X) will be a multi-mission combat ship that will feature weaponry for high-tech anti-land, antiair, anti-surface, and antisubmarine warfare.

In the not-too-distant future, the USS *Constitution* will be not only America's oldest frigate, it will be America's *only* frigate.

▲
The Navy's plan is to eventually replace its guided missile frigates with the next-generation destroyer, designated DD(X).

Glossary

acronym (AK roh nim) — the first letters of words in a phrase or title, joined together to form a "word" such as LAMPS, which stands for Light Airborne MultiPurpose System

bow (BAU) — the front part of a ship

class (KLAS) — a group of ships manufactured to the same, or very similar, specifications, such as the *Perry* class of guided missile frigates

combatants (kom BAT untz) — those engaged in combat

commissioning (kuh MISH un ing) — the act of officially placing a ship into U.S. Navy service

cruisers (KRU zurz) — guided missile-carrying warships, the modern versions being slightly larger than, but similar to, guided missile destroyers

decommissioned (DEE kuh MISH und) — for a ship to have been taken out of active service by the U.S. Navy

destroyers (duh STROI urz) — surface warships traditionally used to defend larger, slower ships from submarines (modern destroyers are armed with guided missiles for multi-missions)

displacements (dis PLAY smuntz) — the water displaced by floating ships; the tonnage of the water displaced

hulls (HULZ) — the main frame and body of a ship

nuclear (NYU klee ur) — providing atomic energy in a controlled, powerful way

obsolete (OB suh LEET) — no longer modern or of its former usefulness

stern (STURN) — the rear part of a ship

superstructures (SOO pur STRUK churz) — the major structures built onto and rising above a ship's upper deck

INDEX

FURTHER READING

Wachtel, Roger. *Old Ironsides*. Children's Press, 2003
Dartford, Mark. *Warships*. Lerner, 2004

WEBSITES TO VISIT

http://www.chinfo.navy.mil/navpalib/factfile/ships/ship-ffg.html
http://navysite.de/frigates.htm
http://www.globalsecurity.org/military/systems/ship/frigates.htm

ABOUT THE AUTHOR

Lynn M. Stone is the author and photographer of many children's books. Lynn is a former teacher who travels worldwide to pursue his varied interests.